To ....

For being good.
MERRY CHRISTMAS!
From Santa

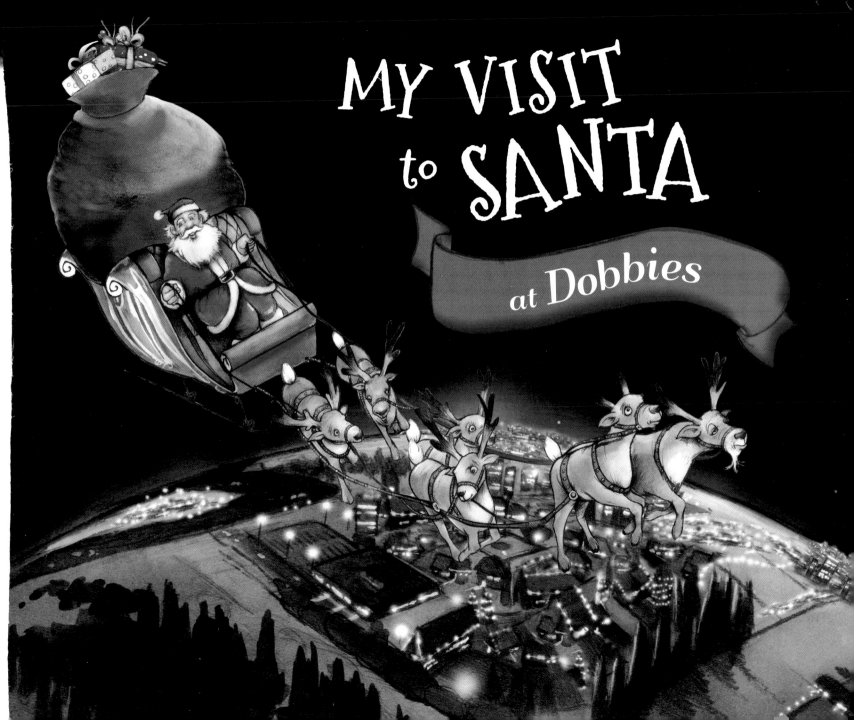

MY VISIT to SANTA

at Dobbies

Dobbies
GARDEN CENTRES
Brighten your day

Written by Katherine Sully
Illustrated by Robert Dunn
Designed by Sarah Allen

This edition published by HOMETOWN WORLD in 2016
Hometown World Ltd
7 Northumberland Buildings
Bath BA1 2JB

www.hometownworld.co.uk

ISBN 978-1-78553-471-3
HTW_PO170616
10 9 8 7 6 5 4 3 2 1

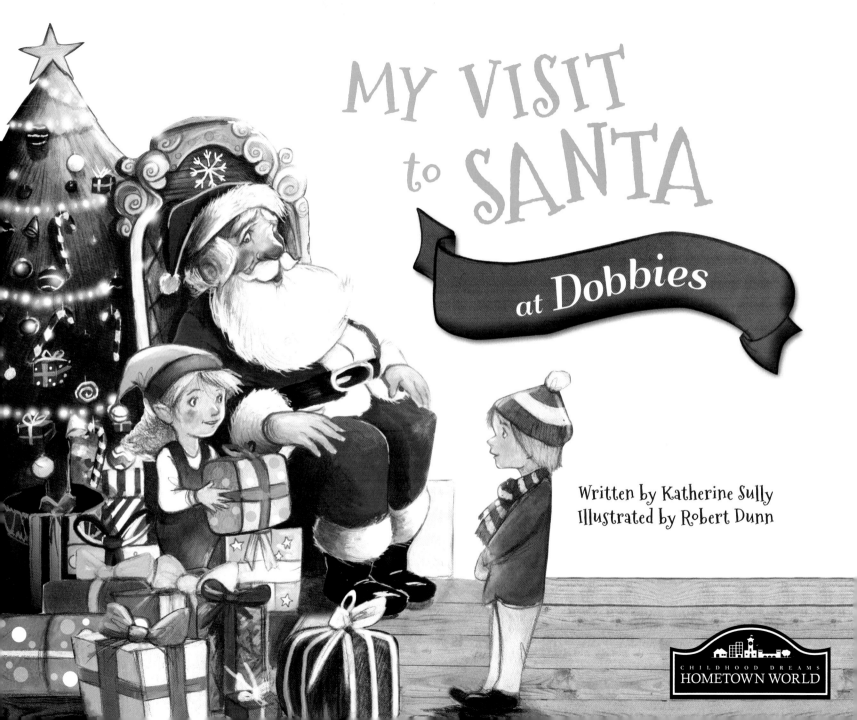

MY VISIT to SANTA

at Dobbies

Written by Katherine Sully
Illustrated by Robert Dunn

CHILDHOOD DREAMS
HOMETOWN WORLD

Dobbies was like a Winter Wonderland, with glittery decorations and sparkly lights everywhere.

The day had finally arrived to see Santa, I was so excited! I was just close enough to glimpse him; he had a fluffy, white beard, big, bushy eyebrows and plump, red cheeks.

I turned to Mum. "What shall I say to Santa?"

"Tell him what Christmas present you're hoping for," she smiled.

SANTA
THIS WAY

"I can't **wait** for
Christmas Day,"
I squealed.

"Who's next?"

I spun back round to see
Santa's helper smiling at me.
"Santa is ready to meet you,"
he said.

MERRY
CHRISTMAS!

"Hello there!" boomed Santa. "Tell me, have you been good this year?"

"Erm...I think so," I whispered. Santa peered down at me.

"You think so!" chuckled Santa.
"And what do you think you'd
like for Christmas?"

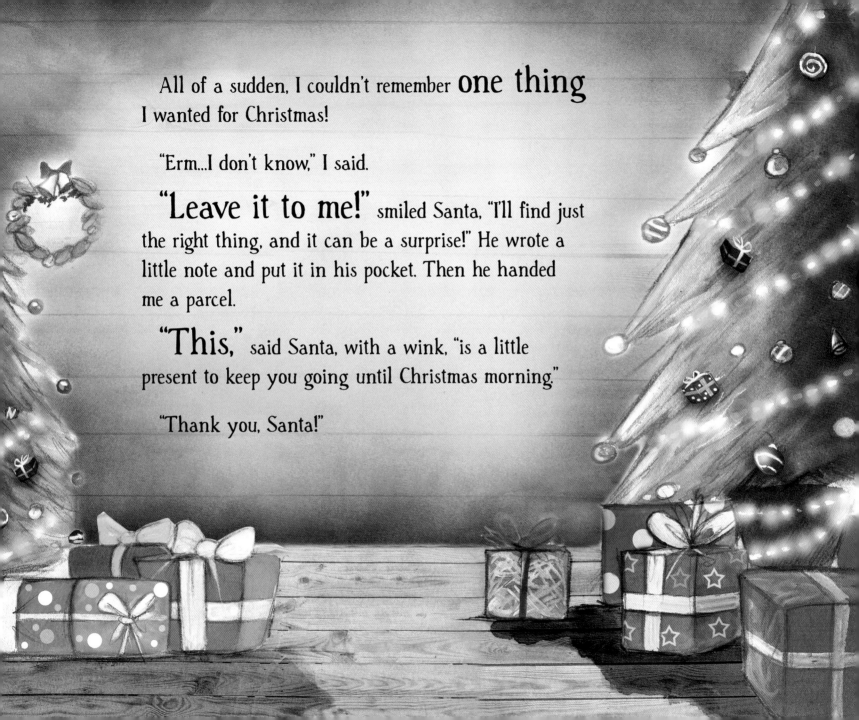

All of a sudden, I couldn't remember **one thing** I wanted for Christmas!

"Erm...I don't know," I said.

"Leave it to me!" smiled Santa, "I'll find just the right thing, and it can be a surprise!" He wrote a little note and put it in his pocket. Then he handed me a parcel.

"This," said Santa, with a wink, "is a little present to keep you going until Christmas morning."

"Thank you, Santa!"

On Christmas Eve, I hung a big sign in the window. I hoped Santa would remember to stop at my house!

Santa, please stop here!

Then I chose a mince pie and Mum poured a little glass of something to put on the table for Santa, with a crunchy carrot for the reindeer.

Last of all, I carefully hung my stocking at the end of my bed and dived under the duvet. I hoped Santa would remember to bring me a surprise present.
I could hardly wait!

Just a few more hours and, at last, it would be Christmas morning! As I closed my eyes, I wondered what Santa was doing right that minute...

Santa was still at the North Pole! He was busy checking all the letters and notes from children around the world to make sure he hadn't missed anyone.

"Well?"

boomed Santa. "Do we have all the presents on our list?" he asked the little old elf.

"Yes, yes," answered the little old elf. "All wrapped and ready to go."

"Splendid!" said Santa.

It's a jolly good thing that Santa has a **magic** sack. Otherwise, he would never be able to fit **all** of the presents for **all** of the children onto his sleigh!

But Santa was looking worried. He patted his pocket and brought out a crumpled note from **Dobbies**.

Santa quickly
gathered up the
surprise parcels and
packed them into the
magic sack on his sleigh.

"Prepare for take-off,"
he said to the sleepy reindeer.
"It's time we were on our way, or
Christmas will be over
before we get there!"

"Hup, hup!"
called Santa in his special reindeer
language. The reindeer skittered and
skidded across the icy snow until,
with a hefty heave, the sleigh
lifted off the ground and
they were flying through
the frosty air.

"Ho, ho, ho!" laughed Santa.
"Here we come!"

As Santa's sleigh flew above the North Pole, icy winds blew them towards Scandinavia.

Then Santa and his reindeer swooped over Germany and on over France.

Before long, Santa's sleigh was whisked back northwards once more, heading towards the UK.

In a blink and a wink, Santa's sleigh was flying across hilltops and mountains, valleys and vales. Santa and his reindeer zoomed over rivers and streams, and zipped over lakes and ponds. All along the way, they visited every city, town, village and farm. Not even the smallest cottage was missed.

Wherever he went, Santa stopped at each house, delivering
presents for all the good little children asleep in their beds.
But, somehow, Santa's magic sack was always full.

He slipped down chimneys, he snuck through air vents,
he shimmied down flues, he even squeezed through pet flaps!

(so that's how
he does it!)

Santa left presents for Abigail, Aiden, Angelica, Arnold, Axl, Azda...
...Zac, Zara, Zeb, Zeke. Every possible name you could think of was on Santa's list.

Finally, Santa and his sleigh were heading towards their final destination. They crisscrossed town from one side to the other, flying above the shopping centre and over the park. Santa was very careful not to miss out anyone. But **still** Santa's magic sack was full!

(He even stopped at the school to leave a little something for the teachers!)

"Last stop!" cried Santa, tugging at the reins. The weary reindeer were very pleased to hear that! They were getting tired and very hungry. They jerked to a halt in a jumbled heap on the rooftop.

And that's when **something woke me up.**

I lay very still and listened.

First, there was a jingling sound, like sleighbells ringing outside my window.

Then, there was a clattering overhead – could it be reindeer hoofs on the roof?

Munch!
Crunch!

(It's a good thing that reindeer run on carrots!)

Huff!
Puff!

Someone was huffing and puffing,
or was I just hearing things?

Then, from inside the house, I thought I heard a rustling sound, like Santa opening his sack.

Did I hear a tinkling? Maybe it was Santa putting parcels under the Christmas tree!

...and I'm sure I heard a slurping and a loud burping, like Santa sipping a little something!

What was that chomping noise? It sounded like Santa munching a mince pie...

I was wide awake now and it was definitely **Christmas** morning – the stocking at the end of my bed was **bursting** with parcels and treats. Tied to the stocking was a label saying:

I hope you enjoy your surprise presents!

Love from Santa

X

There were parcels large and small waiting for me under the Christmas tree.

When I unwrapped them, I couldn't believe my eyes – inside was **exactly** what I'd always wanted.

"Clever Santa!" I shouted up the chimney. "How did you know?"

But Santa wasn't giving away any secrets. He was already flying over **Dobbies** on his way back to the North Pole.